A Papillon Christmas Tale

Text Copyright © 2020 by Kevin J. Brougher & Lisa Santa Cruz
Illustrations Copyright © 2020 by Jessica Warrick

ISBN# 978-1-7340123-4-7
Epub ISBN# 978-1-7340123-6-1
Library of Congress Control Number : 2020908524

Distributed in United States and Canada by Allied Resources - Abilene Texas.
For wholesale and licensing inquiries, please email us at : Questions@MissingPiecePress.com
Missing Piece Press, LLC does not accept unsolicited manuscripts.
Visit : MissingPiecePress.com for information on our other fun products.
LIKE us on Facebook to keep up to date with our new books, games and special offers.
"A little Thinking...a LOT of FUN!" and *"Grandpa Kevin"* are trademarks of Missing Piece Press, LLC.

Other Publications from Missing Piece Press

BOOKS

Thinklers! 1 : *A Collection of Brain Ticklers!*
Thinklers! 2 : *More Brain Ticklers!*
Thinklers! 3 : *Even More Brain Ticklers!*
Thinklers! 4 : *Full-Color Brain Ticklers!*
History Mysteries : *A New Twist on Time-Lines*
State Debate : *50 Unique Playing Cards and 50 Games*
Number Wonders : *A Collection of Amazing Number Facts!*
Dreams, Screams, & JellyBeans! : *Poems for All Ages*
Science Stumpers : *Brain-Busting Scenarios...Solved with Science*
Algebra Summary Sheets : *Posters to Promote Proficiency*
Number Fun! : *A Book of Counting and Numbers for Toddlers*
Who's Waiting for You? : *A Book of Animal Clues for Toddlers*
Reindolphins : *A Christmas Tale*
How the Candy Cane Got Its Stripes : *A Christmas Tale*
Who Says Hoo? : *A Book for Babies & Toddlers*
Grandpa Kevin's... ABC Book : *Really Kinda Strange...*
Grandpa Kevin's...Book of COLOR : *Really Kinda Strange...*
Grandpa Kevin's...Book of NUMBERS : *Really Kinda Strange...*
Grandpa Kevin's... The Three Little Pigs
Grandpa Kevin's...Jack and the Beanstalk
Grandpa Kevin's...Chicken...Chicken
The Arizona Book : *Things to See - Places to Go!*
ARROWS : *A Book of Arrow Puzzles*

GAMES

Frazzle : *A Frenzied Game of Words*
ShanJari : *An African Game of Sequence and Strategy*
Whew! : *Words, Wits, Whims & Woes!*
TooT! : *A Nerdy Little Game*
Blam! : *A Different Card Game*
DICE Blam! : *A Different Dice Game*
Word Nerd : *A Quick-Witted Word Game*
Bunco BUDDIES! : *The BETTER Bunco Game*
Take Twelve : *The Token Taking Game*
CRUMMY : *The Criss-Cross Rummy Game*
Round About : *A Little Thinking - A LOT of FUN!*
Whole Enchilada : *It All Adds up to FUN!*
Besto : *An Animal Matching Game*
Fifty Nifty : *United States Playing Cards & Games*
The Get-to-Know-You Game : *Fun for Families & Friends*
GRID : *The Tic-Tac-Toe - Tac-Toe - Tac-Toe Game*
RUMMAGE : *The Rummy Race Game*
SUM it! : *It All Adds Up to FUN!*
FIDGITS : *Three Fun and Fickle Games of Digits*

A Papillon Christmas Tale

By Kevin J Brougher
Art by Jessica Warrick

Santa's hand wiped his brow
as he gave a low sigh.
He was running behind -
he didn't know why.

Then he pulled out his phone
and with Google he knew,
the world's population
was 8 billion and 2!

With the work load increasing
   the orders not ceasing
      he knew that he needed more help.
Now, who would have guessed
   that the help that was best
      would come in the form of a yelp?

"Yelp yelp", said one pup,
   as the other looked on.
"Yelp, yelp, can we help?
   Can we sing you a song?"

"Can we show you a dance?
   Can we lick clean your toes?
Can we sit in your lap
   and stare nose to nose?"

"What's this? Who are you?
I'm sorry dear dogs,
I'm so overwhelmed -
my mind's in a fog."

"Habanero's my name.
Jalapeño's my sister.
She's younger than me
so at times I assist her.

We're Papillon dogs.
A French - toy breed.
We're quick - we're agile,
we can help with your needs!"

"Hmmm", said Santa.
   "Can you fetch me some yarn?
Can you bring me some paint
   that's out in the barn?"

In a flash they were gone -
   leaping high over toys -
dodging elf girls -
   through the legs of elf boys!

What seemed like a blink,
much less than a minute,
came the dogs and a wagon
with the paint and yarn in it.

"Impressive!", said Santa.
"Impressive for sure!
For my scheduling issues,
you might be the cure!"

"Elves, gather round,
    gather round - listen up!
We are going to get help
    from two Papillon pups!"

"Let them know what you need
    then show them a treat.
They will bring you that part -
    they will find it indeed!"

So, soon little Ben
  and Halley, for short,
were the best little helpers -
  the best kind of support.

They'd find the lost pieces
  of board games and puzzles
and bring them all back
  in their slightly moist muzzles.

From dolls eyes
to truck wheels

to rivets and glue,

not one mistake made.
Okay... just a few.

Habanero took naps
  when his work was complete.
Jalapeño just paused
  to lick a few feet.

Santa was pleased
  with his two pepper team.
It all was near perfect...
  or so it would seem.

One elf began scratching
his head and his chin.
He had lost a work slipper
so, gone was his grin.

He searched high and low
and checked others feet.
But, the slipper was gone -
the pair...incomplete.

And other elf slippers,
socks, and some hats
began disappearing -
as did Santa's cats.

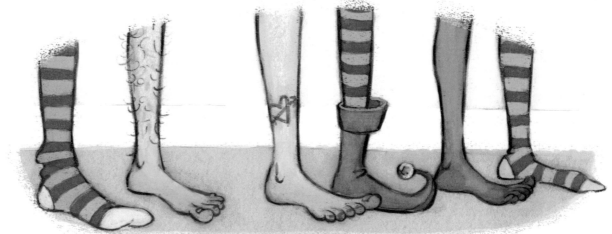

The stockings that hung
by the chimney with care -
one day Santa found them...
no longer there.

Mrs. Claus came to visit
 her husband and elves,
to see finished toys
 on the Christmas shop shelves.
She usually brought with her
cookies and song
 but, this time she screamed...
"My pink panties are gone!"

"Calm down, my sweet dear",
 Santa tried to console.
"I've asked Blitzen and Rudolph
 to be on patrol."

They've reported, now twice,
 and they think they've a clue
on where our stuff is
 and who to pursue."

Then, everyone froze -
each head turned an ear.
Rounding the corner -
two dogs and reindeer!

Jalapeño was dragging
Santa's best silky boxers.
Santa covered his eyes
and 'bout fell off his rocker!

With Rudolph just inches,
just inches behind,
"Get them", he yelled,
"those boxers are mine!"

With his antlers, so gently,
   he snagged Halley's collar.
Elves burst into cheers -
   you could hear Santa holler.

"Good work, my dear Rudolph!
  You've saved us again!
Bring that Papillon here",
  he said rubbing his chin.

Dangling from antlers
  they stood nose to nose.
"Jalapeño", he said,
  "Here's what I propose."

"I see you like fetching
MORE than we need.
I don't know if it's YOU
or just part of your breed."

"But, this just can't go on.
It's a frustrating trend.
We must find a solution.
This thievery must end!"

"Excuse me, dear Santa",
Habanero spoke up,
"My sister's a young
but, big big-hearted pup."

"She meant you no harm -
she loves ALL of you.
So, I've thought of a plan,
here's what I will do.

We'll continue our job
  but... when she starts to walk
to gather some sneakers,
  or slippers or socks,
I'll be right behind her.
  It's a promise I make.
I'll find what it is
  that she's planning to take."

When finally she drops
  the treasure she found -
be it on Santa's couch
  or a foot underground -

I'll bring it right back
  so fast you won't miss!
I'll do this because...
  Jalapeno's...my sis.

Santa was blinking,
  he almost did cry.
"I like this plan.
  Let's give it a try."

So, the Papillon peppers
fetched all that was needed.

And, when Haley got bored
and slowly proceeded
to find a new treasure,
a cap or a glove,

Habanero returned it -
returned it with love.

At the end of the day
 Santa took off his cap -
sat back in his chair
 and opened his lap -

to two loving pups
 who, throughout the day
helped Santa and elves
 make toys for the sleigh.

Santa shared with them stories
of the sleigh riding night.
They immediately thought,
that their help would be right.

So, they wiggled and begged.
They licked and they pleaded.
Santa wisely said, "NO."
Their help was not needed.

But, for years these two Papillons
did what they could.
They'd fetch what was needed
and... put back what they should.

So, if you don't mind
  missing cookies or cups,
YOU might be okay ....
with Papillon pups.

Habanero

Jalapeño

The End

For our full line of books & games,
please visit :
MissingPiecePress.com

Lightning Source UK Ltd.
Milton Keynes UK
UKRC031217231222
414385UK00002B/9